TANTALIZE

KIEREN'S STORY

CYNTHIA LEITICH SMITH

ILLUSTRATED BY MING DOYLE

CANDLEWICK PRESS

QUINCIE P. MORRIS HAS ALWAYS BEEN MY BEST FRIEND. WHEN WE WERE IN MIDDLE SCHOOL, I STARTED TO NOTICE THAT SHE WAS A *GIRL*, TOO.

UM, KIEREN? WHAT IF A TRAIN COMES?

DON'T WORRY. I'LL HEAR IT IN PLENTY OF TIME.

YOU AND YOUR WOLF-MAN SUPERPOWERS!

I'M A HYBRID. THE SON OF A WEREWOLF MOTHER AND A HUMAN FATHER.

HOURS MWThF

HUMAN ONLY

UNLIKE QUINCIE, MOST HUMANS FEAR AND HATE SHAPE-SHIFTERS.

IT'S NOT CLEAR IF WE'RE EVEN CONSIDERED CITIZENS UNDER THE CONSTITUTION.

SO ME, MY MOM, AND MY BABY SIS ARE FIRMLY "IN THE DEN."

IT'S NOT JUST A SUNSET. IT'S A MOONRISE, TOO.

CHOO

KIEREN?

I'D SCREWED UP, DISTRACTED BY THE WAY HER HAND FELT IN MINE. WORSE, I'D BEEN SHOWING OFF.

AHH!

CHOOOO

SHE WAS IN
PAIN, SHOCK.

AND IF I HADN'T MOVED FAST, SHE
COULD'VE DIED BECAUSE OF ME.

THANK GOD I HAD A HEAD START.

THANK GOD MY "WOLF-MAN SUPERPOWERS" INCLUDE STRENGTH AND SPEED.

CHOOOO

9-1-1

NO. . . . WE'D HAVE TO EXPLAIN WHAT HAPPENED. A HOSPITAL MIGHT DETECT YOUR SHIFTER DNA.

QUINCIE WAS STAYING WITH MY FAMILY WHILE HER FOLKS WERE ABROAD.

FORTUNATELY, MY MOM TRAINED AS A HEALER BEFORE LEAVING HER WOLF PACK.

HOW IS SHE?

SLEEPING.

I MANAGED TO SAVE HER HAND. SHE SHOULDN'T HAVE ANY SIGNIFICANT LOSS OF MOBILITY.

KIEREN, YOU WERE BOTH LUCKY TODAY.

I DIDN'T WANT TO RISK EVER HURTING QUINCIE AGAIN.

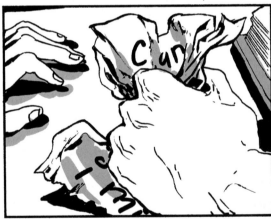

THAT WINTER, QUINCIE'S MOM AND DAD DIED IN A CAR ACCIDENT.

I *HAD* TO BE THERE FOR HER. SHE NEEDED ME.

BUT I CAN'T STAY IN AUSTIN FOREVER. IT'S TRADITIONAL FOR URBAN WOLVES TO JOIN A PACK AT EIGHTEEN.

welcome to FAT LORENZ

AND BECAUSE I CAN'T CONTROL MY SHIFT, I MIGHT HAVE TO GO EVEN SOONER.

BIOLOGY II

IT'S HARD TO IMAGINE. WE'LL BE SENIORS THIS YEAR. BUT I STILL HAVEN'T TOLD QUINCIE THAT I'LL HAVE TO LEAVE.

MY MOTHER IMMIGRATED TO AUSTIN, TEXAS, FROM IRELAND, AND FROM A WOLF PACK TO THE HUMAN WORLD.

SHE STAYED BECAUSE OF MY FATHER. SHE'S A ROMANTIC, BELIEVE IT OR NOT.

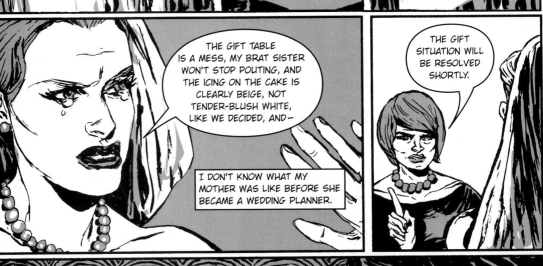

THE GIFT TABLE IS A MESS, MY BRAT SISTER WON'T STOP POUTING, AND THE ICING ON THE CAKE IS CLEARLY BEIGE, NOT TENDER-BLUSH WHITE, LIKE WE DECIDED, AND—

I DON'T KNOW WHAT MY MOTHER WAS LIKE BEFORE SHE BECAME A WEDDING PLANNER.

THE GIFT SITUATION WILL BE RESOLVED SHORTLY.

BUT SHE'S ALWAYS BEEN FIERCE IN A CRISIS.

KIEREN?

GO ASK THE BRIDE'S BRAT SISTER TO DANCE.

SHE ALWAYS DEMANDS 100 PERCENT OBEDIENCE.

LUCKY YOU.

AS FOR THE ICING, IT IS PRECISELY THE SHADE YOU SELECTED AT THE FIFTH TASTING.

BUT—

THIS IS YOUR SPECIAL NIGHT. DO YOU WANT TO GO ENJOY IT, OR DO YOU WANT TO CONTINUE WHINING TO ME?

I GET PAID EITHER WAY.

AND THIS RUN-OF-THE-MILL BRIDEZILLA STANDS ZERO CHANCE AGAINST MY ALPHA BITCH MAMA WOLF.

TONIGHT QUINCIE AND I CAME ALONG AS BACKUP. MOST NIGHTS QUINCIE WORKS AT HER FAMILY'S RESTAURANT. BUT IT'S CLOSED FOR REMODELING.

SHE'S MORE OF A T-SHIRT AND JEANS KIND OF GIRL.

USUALLY.

KIEREN?

NOW.

EXCUSE ME.

YOUR MOM NEEDS HELP HAULING SOME PLASTERED STEPUNCLE TO HIS CAB.

MY MOTHER COULD BENCH-PRESS A REFRIGERATOR, BUT IT'S ALL ABOUT APPEARANCES.

SPEAKING OF WHICH, QUINCIE LOOKS, AND SMELLS, AMAZING.

IT TAKES EFFORT NOT TO STARE AT HER, ALL MY WILL NOT TO REACH FOR HER.

THEN . . .

SHE REACHES FOR ME.

IT'S THE FIRST TIME I'VE EVER REALLY HELD HER.

THE FIRST TIME IN ALL THESE YEARS.

MAY I CUT IN?

OH, I'M SORRY. WE JUST—

QUINCIE TOLD ME YOU NEEDED—

SWEEP THE PARTY PERIMETER, QUINCIE.

REPORT BACK IN THREE MINUTES.

KIEREN.

WE WEREN'T—

DON'T MAKE IT ANY HARDER ON HER. OR ON YOU, EITHER.

REMEMBER, SOONER OR LATER . . .

IT'S NOT LIKE I COULD FORGET.

I'D FEEL A LOT BETTER ABOUT SOMEDAY LEAVING IF I HAD CLUE ONE ABOUT THE PACK.

WHERE IT IS.

WHAT IT'S LIKE.

ANYTHING.

BUT MOM REFUSES TO FILL ME IN.

I KNOW BETTER THAN TO ASK AGAIN.

HAVE YOU TOLD QUINCIE YET?

THAT I'M LEAVING?

I WILL.

SOON.

11

A WEEK LATER

QUINCIE'S UNCLE DAVIDSON REMODELED THEIR FAMILY'S ITALIAN RESTAURANT TO INCORPORATE A VAMPIRE THEME AND CHANGED THE NAME FROM FAT LORENZO'S TO SANGUINI'S.

IT'S SUPPOSED TO BE ALL IN FUN. BUT VAMPIRES ARE REAL ENOUGH. DEMONIC. DEADLY.

I'M MEETING QUINCIE HERE WHEN SHE GETS OFF WORK.

TONIGHT I'M FINALLY GOING TO TELL HER ABOUT THE WOLF PACK.

MOM IS RIGHT. SHE DESERVES TO KNOW.

I SMELL SCALLOPS AND GARLIC.

I SMELL MARINARA AND URINE . . .

BLOOD AND WINE.

IT'S CHEF VAGGIO!

QUINCIE . . . WHERE ARE YOU? QUINCIE!

QUINCIE!

THANK GOD YOU'RE OKAY.

YOU'RE A MESS. WHERE'S . . .

WHERE'S VAGGIO?

VAGGIO?

13

VAGGIO BIANCHI WAS A HARDWORKING, FUN-LOVING GUY . . .

A LIFELONG FRIEND TO ME AND LIKE A GRANDFATHER TO QUINCIE.

I TRIED TO HELP HIM, BUT IT WAS TOO LATE.

OUR CONVERSATION ABOUT THE WOLF PACK WILL HAVE TO WAIT.

I WAS JUST IN THE NEXT ROOM.

I KNOW.

DO YOU THINK THE KILLER IS STILL IN THERE?

I DON'T KNOW.

WHERE'S QUINCIE?

YOUR GIRLFRIEND?

MY *BEST* FRIEND.

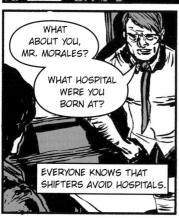

WHAT ABOUT YOU, MR. MORALES?

WHAT HOSPITAL WERE YOU BORN AT?

EVERYONE KNOWS THAT SHIFTERS AVOID HOSPITALS.

LONE WOLVES USE MIDWIVES AND HOUSE-CALL DOCTORS.

WOLF PACKS HAVE THEIR OWN HEALERS. LIKE MY MOTHER WOULD'VE BEEN IF SHE HADN'T LEFT.

SHOULDN'T MY PARENTS BE HERE BY NOW?

KIEREN'S ROOM, THE NEXT DAY

I MET CLYDE AND TRAVIS IN THE LOOSE NETWORK OF AUSTIN WEREPEOPLE.

WE BROUGHT PIZZA IN HONOR OF VAGGIO.

AND DOGGIE TREATS FOR BRAZOS.

CLYDE IS A WEREOPOSSUM.

TRAVIS, A WEREARMADILLO.

LIKE WOLVES, THEIR SPECIES ARE OFFSHOOTS OF ANCESTORS THAT CAN BE TRACED TO THE ICE AGE, A TIME OF GIANT MAMMALS.

WEREPEOPLE, NOT SHIFTERS, IS THE PREFERRED TERM FOR US. EVEN THOUGH WERE MEANS MAN.

MAN-PERSON IS REDUNDANT, BUT I'D RATHER BE CALLED THAT THAN MONSTER.

IT'LL SUCK COMPARED TO HIS PIZZA.

IT'S THE THOUGHT THAT MATTERS. RIGHT, KIEREN?

THEY DIDN'T KNOW VAGGIO LIKE I DID. BUT THEY WERE FAT LORENZO'S REGULARS.

RIGHT.

VAGGIO'S MURDER IS ALL OVER THE NEWS.

NOT JUST IN AUSTIN. IT'S ON EVERY TWENTY-FOUR-HOUR TV CHANNEL.

YOU DIDN'T DO IT, RIGHT?

HE MEANS, UH . . .

I TRY NOT TO LET ON THAT THE QUESTION BOTHERS ME. THEY MAY BE MY FRIENDS, BUT THEY'RE ALSO PREY SHIFTERS.

THEY DON'T KNOW THAT I'M A HYBRID OR THAT I'VE NEVER FULLY TRANSFORMED BEFORE.

I JUST DISCOVERED THE BODY.

SO WHO—OR WHAT—DID IT?

DALLAS, 1963. I KNOW.

BUT THEY'RE HARD TO I.D.

AFTER THEIR FIRST KILL, THEY CAN HIDE BEHIND HUMANLIKE FACES.

YIKES.

AND FORGET WHAT YOU MAY HAVE SEEN AT THE MOVIES; SUNLIGHT DOESN'T DESTROY VAMPIRES.

IT JUST TEMPORARILY WEAKENS THEM.

THEY CAN REFLECT, TOO. SORT OF.

SO ANY EASY MEANS OF DETECTION ARE OUT.

IT TAKES ABOUT A MONTH AFTER A HUMAN IS EXPOSED TO VAMPIRE BLOOD—BY DRINKING OR TRANSFUSION— TO TRIGGER A TRANSFORMATION.

BUT VAMPS KILL TO FEED. WHY MURDER VAGGIO LIKE THAT?

IT'S A SETUP.

YOU THINK?

IT WOULD BE A HELL OF A COINCIDENCE IF THE NEXT PERSON THROUGH THAT DOOR JUST HAPPENED TO BE A WEREWOLF.

BEDTIME

THE MOON HAS A CERTAIN PULL. . . .

NORMALLY, A WOLF CAN CONTROL HIS SHIFT.

BUT SINCE I'M A HYBRID, IT'S DIFFERENT FOR ME.

I'VE NEVER BEEN ABLE TO FULLY SHIFT, AND I ONLY WENT PARTWAY THAT ONE TIME, AT THE RAILROAD TRACKS.

SO, ON SOME LEVEL, I'M UNSTABLE.

THAT'S WHY QUINCIE GOT HURT.

I'M BETTING MOST TEEN WOLVES DON'T HAVE WATER BEDS. IF THE CLAWS COME OUT, WELL, SO MUCH FOR MOM'S BERBER CARPETING.

IT'S A REMINDER TO STAY LOCKED DOWN.

EVEN IN MY DREAMS.

VAGGIO LIVED SO WELL. HE SHOULDN'T HAVE DIED IN SUCH A TERRIBLE WAY.

THE WAY I SEE IT, ANYONE CONNECTED TO HIM MIGHT BE A SUSPECT, OR IN DANGER, OR BOTH.

THE AUSTIN POLICE DEPARTMENT SEEMS TO AGREE.

QUINCIE'S UNCLE DAVIDSON BROUGHT HIS GIRLFRIEND, RUBY, TO THE MEMORIAL SERVICE.

I'VE ONLY MET HER IN PASSING A COUPLE OF TIMES.

SHE'S A "LIVING VAMPIRE," A HUMAN WANNABE.

A PATHETIC, WALKING CLICHÉ.

QUINCIE'S PARENTS WERE MY GODPARENTS. I WONDER: DID THEY EVER TELL DAVIDSON THAT I'M A WOLF?

VAGGIO'S MANY LADY FRIENDS PAY THEIR RESPECTS TO QUINCIE.

HE LOVED YOU.

TALKED ABOUT YOU ALL THE TIME.

LIGHT OF HIS LIFE.

PRIDE AND JOY.

GRANDDAUGHTER HE NEVER HAD.

HELL OF A GUY, VAGGIO.

I CAN'T EVEN HANDLE ONE GIRL.

22

QUINCIE, I HATE TO BRING THIS UP, BUT THE MURDERER MIGHT—

DON'T TALK ABOUT THAT. NOT HERE.

WHERE, THEN?

IT'S . . . I GET THAT THE POLICE CAN ONLY DO SO MUCH.

WHEN I GO BACK TO THE RESTAURANT, I'M TAKING GRAMPA CRIMI'S .45 WITH ME.

NO WAY IN HELL. SOMEBODY COULD USE IT AGAINST YOU.

AND EVEN IF YOU WERE A SHARPSHOOTER, I DON'T THINK A GUN WOULD HELP.

I'M SCARED, OKAY?

OKAY.

I LOVE YOU, YOU KNOW.

I PLAY IT OFF LIKE SHE MEANS "AS A FRIEND." IT'S A HORRIBLE THING TO DO TO HER.

TO BOTH OF US.

ESPECIALLY TODAY.

WHEN I WAS EIGHT, MOM TOLD ME THAT THERE ARE TWO WAYS INTO A WOLF PACK: SCHOLARSHIP OR ATHLETICISM.

http://www.vampirestockade.com

CHECKOUT cart

Bell..........................
Buckthorn.................. 1
Candle 1
Carrot seeds 8
Holy Cross 1
Crucifix 4
Dehumidifier 4
Humidifier.................. 2
Box of wafers.............. 2

Gongs ....
Holy water.................. 1
Mustard seeds............. 9
Prayer wheel............... 1
Prayer flag................. 3
Dried red peppers 3
Star of David.............. 5

I'M STRONGER AND FASTER THAN A HUMAN, BUT NOT AS STRONG OR AS FAST AS A FULL WOLF.

SO I BEGAN MY STUDIES.

NOW IT'S NOT JUST ABOUT THE PACK. IT'S ABOUT SOLVING VAGGIO'S MURDER.

I WANT THE KILLER TO PAY. I WANT TO CLEAR MY NAME. I WANT TO RUN FREE AND HOWL TO THE HEAVENS.

BUT MOST OF ALL, I NEED TO MAKE SURE QUINCIE IS SAFE.

MY SISTER, MEGHAN, IS THE WORLD'S CUTEST CUB.

STORY?

AND IT DOESN'T HURT THAT SHE WORSHIPS ME.

I'LL MISS SEEING MEGHAN GROW UP, BUT EVENTUALLY, SHE'LL JOIN THE WOLF PACK, TOO.

QUINCIE STOPPING BY IS NOTHING UNUSUAL.

GRRR

- BUT SHE SMELLS NERVOUS TONIGHT.

GRRRUFF

RUFFRFFF RRRR

I THINK SHE WANTS TO KISS ME.

GRUFF! RUFF!

I KNOW I WANT HER TO KISS ME.

GRRR

BUT IT'LL BE HARD ENOUGH TO LEAVE QUINCIE.

WITHOUT STARTING SOMETHING WE CAN'T FINISH.

RUFF! RUFF!

27

IT'S NOT YOU.
YOU'RE . . .
I JUST . . .
I DON'T WANT
TO HURT YOU.

AGAIN.

GRUFF! RUFF RUF! GR

I GUESS THERE'S NEVER GOING
TO BE A GOOD TIME TO SAY THIS.

I THINK VAMPIRES
KILLED VAGGIO.

UM, KIEREN,
I WAS IN THE KITCHEN.
IT LOOKED LIKE—

I'M UPSET BECAUSE OF WHAT YOUR MAMA TOLD ME DOWNSTAIRS. THAT YOU'LL BE LEAVING SOON TO JOIN A WOLF PACK. LEAVING *FOREVER*.

THAT'S WHY YOU'VE BEEN HOLDING BACK ON US, ISN'T IT?

RUFF! RR RUFF! RI

I SHOULD'VE KNOWN THIS WAS GOING TO HAPPEN.

I STILL HAVE NO IDEA WHAT TO SAY.

GRUFF! RRRR

MOM ALREADY LEFT TO MEET WITH A BRIDE. DAD WON'T BE HOME FROM HIS FACULTY DINNER UNTIL LATER TONIGHT.

BRAZOS WOULDN'T BARK LIKE THAT AT FAMILY.

I THINK SOMEONE'S OUTSIDE.

CHECK ON MEGHAN.

31

I WISH MY SENSES WERE AS GOOD AS MY MOTHER'S.

MALE. SMELLED LIKE SOME KIND OF SPICE. GONE NOW, I THINK. OR MAYBE IT WAS A SHE . . . ? OR A CAT?

A CAT?

A WERECAT, I MEAN, BUT I DON'T SAY SO. I'VE THROWN ENOUGH AT QUINCIE FOR ONE DAY.

CATS AND DOGS DON'T GET ALONG.

LATER THAT NIGHT

WHERE DID MY MOTHER CULL TOGETHER THESE WOLF STUDIES MATERIALS FROM ANYWAY? DID SHE TAKE THEM WHEN SHE LEFT THE PACK?

IF BEING A SCHOLAR MATTERS, THERE MUST BE A COLLEGE OR THINK TANK OR SOMETHING AT THE WOLF PACK. BUT HAS MY MAKESHIFT LIBRARY PREPARED ME? HALF OF THE BOOKS ARE WRITTEN IN LANGUAGES I DON'T KNOW.

DAD'S HOME . . .

YOU'RE STILL AWAKE?

QUINCIE CAME BY EARLIER. MOM TOLD HER I WAS LEAVING.

I WANTED QUINCIE TO HEAR IT FROM ME.

HAVE YOU TALKED TO YOUR MOTHER YET?

NOPE.

I WOULD NEVER—

NO, BECAUSE THERE WILL BE NO TEMPTATION.

WHO WOULD I TELL? QUINCIE? SHE ALREADY KNOWS MORE ABOUT WOLVES THAN MOST HUMAN BEINGS.

THIS ISN'T ABOUT WHAT'S FAIR, KIEREN. IT'S ABOUT PROTECTING HER. PROTECTING A LOT OF PEOPLE. I KNOW MORE THAN I SHOULD.

BUT QUINCIE ISN'T PREJUDICED AGAINST SHIFTERS. SHE WOULD NEVER GO TO THE MEDIA OR THE AUTHORITIES.

BESIDES, IT'S NOT LIKE THE TRUTH ABOUT WOLVES IS THAT SCARY.

IS IT?

AS YOUR LAWYER, I'M TELLING YOU: STAY AWAY FROM SANGUINI'S.

I CAN'T. MY BEST FRIEND—

HER, TOO.

BUZZ

I HAVE TO TAKE THIS. IF YOU'LL EXCUSE ME . . .

CLICK

I CAN'T JUST RUN AWAY. QUINCIE—

WE'LL LOOK OUT FOR HER. *YOU* NEED TO THINK ABOUT YOUR FUTURE, ABOUT—

MEGHAN. *I KNOW.* I'M NOT STUPID. I'M NOT GOING TO DO ANYTHING THAT COULD EXPOSE THE FAMILY. I'VE GOT ZERO INTENTION OF SPENDING THE REST OF MY LIFE BEHIND BARS.

BUT QUINCIE LOVED VAGGIO. FIRST HER PARENTS, NOW THIS. CAN'T WE GIVE HER A LITTLE MORE TIME?

I DON'T MENTION THAT I'M TRYING TO SOLVE THE MURDER.

ALL RIGHT, BUT WHEN WE SAY IT'S TIME . . .

YOU'LL BE CAREFUL?

DELIVERY ENTRANCE →

QUINCIE'S UNCLE HIRED A CHEF TO REPLACE VAGGIO.

HIS NAME IS BRAD, AND HE'S NEW IN TOWN.

I DON'T LIKE THE LOOK OF HIM.

I DON'T LIKE THE WAY HE LOOKS AT HER.

MITCH IS A NEIGHBORHOOD FIXTURE.

PRO-CHOICE AMISH LAID-OFF TECH WORKER NEEDS BOOZE $

YOU GOTTA KNOW. COPS TALKED TO ME, HAD LOTS OF QUESTIONS. SO MANY. ASKED ABOUT YOU. I, I TOLD 'EM YOU WAS GOOD KIDS.

THEY'RE JUST DOING THEIR JOBS.

WATCH, WATCH . . . TAKE CARE. CARE FOR HER, BOY.

PRO CHO LAID OFF NEEDS B

39

I TUTOR JOEY MARTINEZ AFTER SCHOOL. IT'S ONE OF THOSE THINGS I DO TO LOOK LIKE A NORMAL HUMAN GUY. LIKE TUTORING IS A BIG PRIORITY FOR NORMAL HUMAN GUYS. IT'S MY MOTHER'S IDEA.

JOEY'S NOT DUMB. HE'S JUST NOT AS INTO SCHOOL AS HE IS INTO VARIOUS ILLEGAL ACTIVITIES I DON'T WANT TO KNOW ABOUT.

JOEY'S THE ONLY PERSON WHOSE OPINION OF ME WENT UP AFTER WORD GOT AROUND THAT I'D DISCOVERED VAGGIO'S BODY.

QUÉ ONDA, MAN? DON'T YOU GOT SOMEWHERE BETTER TO BE?

DON'T WE ALL?

IT'S TOO BAD. IF I WASN'T A WEREWOLF, AND HE WASN'T A CRIMINAL, WE MIGHT'VE BEEN FRIENDS.

IS QUINCIE THERE?

NO, SHE'S AT WORK.

WHAT TIME WILL SHE BE BACK?

I'LL TELL HER YOU CALLED.

DAVIDSON IS OVERPROTECTIVE OF HIS NIECE, ESPECIALLY WHEN IT COMES TO GUYS.

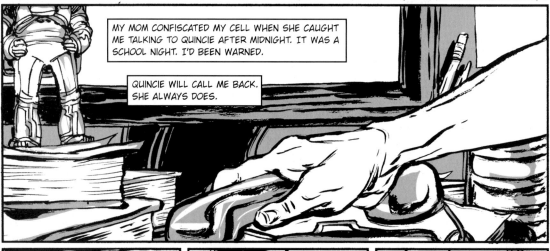

MY MOM CONFISCATED MY CELL WHEN SHE CAUGHT ME TALKING TO QUINCIE AFTER MIDNIGHT. IT WAS A SCHOOL NIGHT. I'D BEEN WARNED.

QUINCIE WILL CALL ME BACK. SHE ALWAYS DOES.

WHO *IS* THIS BRAD GUY? HE APPEARS OUT OF NOWHERE. HE'S GOT VAGGIO'S JOB—PLAYING THE VAMPIRE CHEF. HE *BENEFITED* FROM THE MURDER.

HE'S SUDDENLY WITH QUINCIE ALL THE TIME. PREPARING FOR THE GRAND REOPENING, OR SO SHE SAYS.

AFTER HE LEAVES THE NEXT NIGHT, I FOLLOW BRAD TO SIXTH STREET.

YOU GOT I.D.?

I, UH—

THE GOOD NEWS IS, SHE ISN'T QUINCIE.

WHERE DID THEY GO?

Sanguini's

I COULD CATCH UP WITH QUINCIE RIGHT AWAY, BUT NOT WITHOUT USING WOLF SPEED.

AND I CAN'T RISK SOMEONE SEEING ME DO THAT.

QUINCIE.

SHE CAN'T HEAR ME.

I CAN'T YELL. I'LL WAKE THE NEIGHBORS.

QU–

YOU NEVER WALK ALONE AT NIGHT.

I KNOW.

MY UNCLE'S OUT WITH RUBY. WANNA COME IN?

I'M OH-SO TEMPTED TO SAY YES.

BUT I CAN SMELL WINE ON HER BREATH.

IT'S A SCHOOL NIGHT, HONEY.

DAVIDSON CAME HOME EARLY FOR A CHANGE.

GAME NIGHT

I'M NOT WHAT PEOPLE THINK OF AS A FOOTBALL KIND OF GUY, BUT I LIKE THE SPORT.

I LIKE THAT THERE ARE RULES AND REFEREES. I LIKE THAT YOU KNOW IF YOU'RE WINNING OR LOSING.

I COULD NEVER RISK PLAYING, THOUGH. COULDN'T TAKE TIME OFF FROM MY WOLF STUDIES. COULDN'T RISK HURTING SOMEONE.

HEY, KIEREN. YOU SEEN LISA?

LISA CYRUS, SHE MEANS. NICE GIRL, LISA. LIVES DOWN THE STREET FROM ME. SHE AND TANDI ARE BEST FRIENDS.

SHE TOOK OFF TO GRAB NACHOS, BUT THAT WAS OVER AN HOUR AGO.

SORRY. IF I RUN INTO HER, I'LL LET HER KNOW YOU'RE LOOKING.

WHAT A DOLL.

THE VAMPIRE CHEF.

WHAT'S HE DOING HERE? BESIDES OGLING HIGH-SCHOOL GIRLS.

I DON'T BELIEVE WE'VE FORMALLY MET, BUT CERTAINLY WE'VE SEEN EACH OTHER AROUND. OR AT LEAST, YOU'VE SEEN ME.

MEANING WHAT, EXACTLY?

HE KNOWS I'VE BEEN SPYING ON HIM.

I HAVE EYES IN THE SKY.

QUINCIE DIDN'T MENTION THAT YOU WERE A POET.

POET, CHEF, I'M WHATEVER SHE NEEDS ME TO BE.

BUT YOU, YOU'RE SOMETHING ELSE, AREN'T YOU?

DOES HE KNOW I'M A WOLF? WHO TOLD HIM? DAVIDSON?

NOT QUINCIE. SHE WOULDN'T BETRAY ME.

WOULD SHE?

THIS *BABOSO* BOTHERIN' YOU?

YOU KNOW, COUNT SANGUINI, QUINCIE DIDN'T MENTION THAT YOU WERE A BIGOT.

I'M JUST WONDERING WHOSE SIDE HE'S ON.

YOU HERE TO CHEER FOR WATERLOO HIGH? BECAUSE IF NOT, YOU BELONG ACROSS THE STADIUM.

EASY, BOY, I'M JUST VISITING, TAKING IN THE LOCAL CULTURE. THIS IS A PUBLIC SCHOOL, AND AFTER ALL, I'M A TAX-PAYING—

A TAX-PAYING WHAT?

SCORE ONE FOR THE HOME TEAM.

QUINCIE

ME

SUSPECTS

RUBY

DAVIDSON

?

BRAD

THAT RUBY IS YOWZA GORGEOUS. WE'RE TALKING RED-HOT SMOKIN'.

CLYDE AND TRAVIS GOT DISHWASHER JOBS AT SANGUINI'S. THEY'RE MY ON-SITE EYES AND EARS.

SHE CREEPS ME OUT.

SHE'S *TRYING* TO CREEP YOU OUT. IT'S SEXY.

YOU WORRY ME SOMETIMES.

BUT THE "VAMPIRE CHEF" IS ANOTHER STORY. KIEREN, MAN, HE'S ALL OVER YOUR GIRLFRIEND.

WHAT DO YOU MEAN "ALL OVER"?

SHE'S ALWAYS WITH HIM. ALL THEY DO IS BRAINSTORM ABOUT THE NEW MENU AND HOW TO FIX HIS BLAH IMAGE FOR THE RELAUNCH.

BUT THAT'S . . . WORK, RIGHT?

IT'S QUINCIE'S JOB TO HELP MAKE OVER THE NEW CHEF SO HE CAN PLAY A CONVINCING VAMPIRE FOR THE CROWD. THE LAUNCH PARTY IS IN LESS THAN THREE WEEKS.

THEY'VE BEEN SHOPPING FOR HIS CLOTHES.

THEY'RE . . . KIEREN, THEY'RE PRACTICALLY INSEPARABLE.

EXCEPT WHEN SHE'S AT SCHOOL.

WHY WOULD SHE–?

WELL, SHE KNOWS YOU'RE DITCHING TOWN ANY DAY NOW.

SHE'S STILL FLOORED BY VAGGIO'S MURDER.

AND YOU DISCOVERED HIS BODY.

CLYDE DOESN'T USE THE WORDS *SUSPECT* OR *WEREWOLF*.

HE DOESN'T HAVE TO.

I DON'T KNOW HOW BRAD REALIZED I'VE BEEN FOLLOWING HIM. I'M NOT ABOUT TO BACK OFF NOW, THOUGH THE BAR DISTRICT FEELS A LOT MORE LIKE HIS TURF THAN MINE.

HEY, KIEREN! KIEREN! WHATCHA DOIN' DOWNTOWN? YOU LIKE, LIKE THE NIGHTLIFE?

SHH!

SHH! THAT'S RIGHT, SHH! TOO MANY PEOPLE. TOO MUCH NOISE. EVERYONE IS A-SCARED TO BE ALONE. EVERYONE IS, IS SCARY.

CONSERVATIVE TRANSGENDER VETERA

MITCH . . .

IT'S NO USE. BRAD'S SEEN ME.

THAT'S WEIRD. IT'S UNLOCKED.

YOU MIGHT TRY KNOCKING NEXT TIME.

WHERE'S QUINCIE?

SHE'S CURRENTLY OCCUPIED.

OH, YEAH? WHERE'S LISA?

WHO? I DON'T KNOW WHAT YOU'RE TALKING ABOUT. LOOK, THE RESTAURANT IS CLOSED.

I'VE ALWAYS BEEN WELCOME HERE. QUINCIE'S PARENTS WERE MY GODPARENTS. DO YOU WANT TO EXPLAIN TO HER—?

DO YOU WANT TO EXPLAIN TO THE POLICE WHY YOU'VE BEEN STALKING ME?

STALKING YOU?

OKAY, SORT OF.

I DON'T KNOW. DO I?

KIEREN, WAIT! DON'T BE MAD.

LOOK, IT'S JUST LIKE THIS BECAUSE WE'RE GETTING READY TO REOPEN. IN A FEW WEEKS, EVERYTHING WILL BE BACK TO NORMAL.

I WANT TO SAY THAT IN A FEW WEEKS I COULD BE IN JAIL, COULD BE RUNNING WITH THE PACK, COULD BE A DEAD DOG.

I HATE TO BEG.

CHIPS AND QUESO?

YOU'RE HUNGRY. . . .

IF SHE OFFERS HIS COOKING, SO HELP ME—

QUESO SOUNDS DELICIOUS.

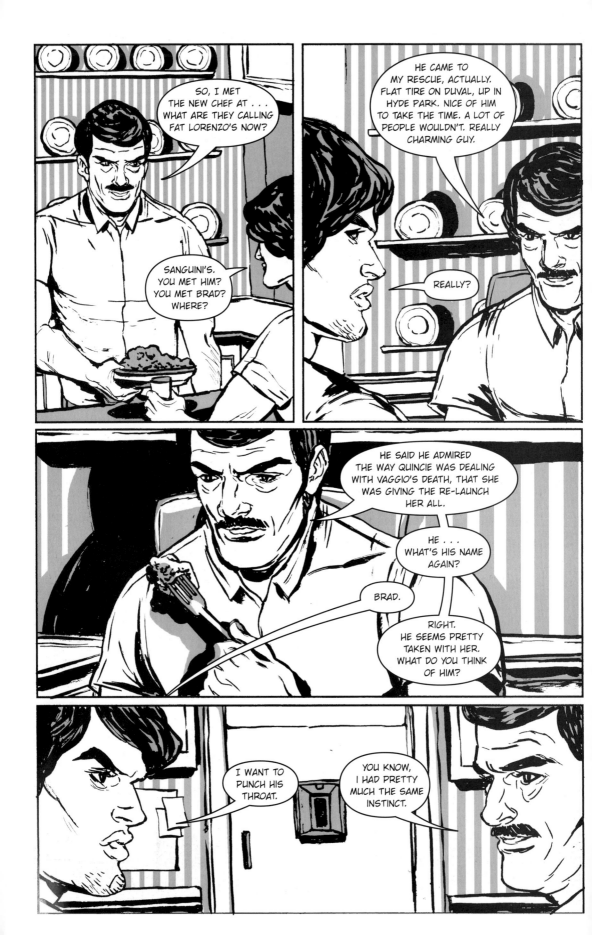

HEY, YOU! KID!

THE GUY'S HUGE.

YOU'RE MEARA MORALES'S BOY?

THAT'S RIGHT.

I'M ZALESKI. HOW ABOUT I WALK YOU OUT TO YOUR TRUCK?

I, UH, HAVE A LAWYER AND . . .

I'VE ALREADY GIVEN MY STATEMENT.

GOOD. THAT'S GOOD.

BUT THE SYSTEM DOESN'T ALWAYS PLAY FAIR, DOES IT?

HE'S A SHIFTER. SOME KIND OF REALLY *BIG* SHIFTER.

SO, YOU GOT ANY THEORIES ON THE MISSING STUDENTS?

DO YOU?

I KNOW THEY'RE GONE. I KNOW THEY GO TO SCHOOL HERE AND SO DO YOU. I KNOW YOU'RE ALSO THE ONE WHO FOUND THAT ITALIAN CHEF DEAD. WHAT'S IT BEEN, THREE WEEKS?

GREAT. NOW THEY THINK I'M A SERIAL KILLER.

YOUR POINT BEING?

I MET YOUR MOM YEARS AGO AT U.T. WE USED TO GO OUT SOMETIMES. SHE EVER MENTION ME?

NO.

I BET SHE'S A FINE MOTHER. I BET SHE DID A GOOD JOB WITH YOU KIDS. I BET YOU BOTH TURN OUT TO BE MODEL CITIZENS. YOU HEAR WHAT I'M SAYIN'?

I'M NOT SURE WHAT DIFFERENCE IT MAKES. BUT I THINK I HAVE A FRIEND ON THE POLICE FORCE.

TEACHER'S PET.

THIS IS MY SECOND AP ENGLISH CLASS WITH MRS. LEVY. I HAD HER JUNIOR YEAR, TOO.

I'VE ALWAYS DONE WELL IN SCHOOL. IT'S KEY IN PREPARING FOR THE PACK.

WHO CAN TELL ME ABOUT OVID'S METAMORPHOSES?

BUT SHE MAKES ME FEEL LIKE THERE COULD BE MORE TO MY FUTURE. LIKE I COULD BE A WRITER, FOR REAL.

QUINCIE DOESN'T USUALLY GET MINUSES. SHE'S NOT A STRAIGHT-A STUDENT LIKE ME, BUT SHE'S ALWAYS MADE HONOR ROLL.

BABES AND BIKES

HOW OLD IS BRAD, ANYWAY?

TWENTY-TWO? TWENTY-THREE?

PERVERT.

QUINCIE AND I CELEBRATE THE MEMORY OF HER PARENTS EVERY YEAR ON THEIR WEDDING ANNIVERSARY, HERE AT THEIR GRAVES.

IT REMINDS ME WHY, EVEN AFTER VAGGIO'S MURDER, SANGUINI'S IS SO IMPORTANT TO HER. THE RESTAURANT HELPS KEEP THEIR MEMORY ALIVE.

FOR A LONG TIME, WE TALK ABOUT HER MOM AND DAD. WE LAUGH AND REMEMBER.

THEN I'M ABOUT TO BRING UP SCHOOL WHEN . . .

I WAS JUST THINKING ABOUT VAGGIO BEING BURIED IN CHICAGO.

THAT'S WHERE HIS FAMILY IS.

BUT WE'RE HIS FAMILY, TOO, IN A WAY. I USED TO TELL HIM EVERYTHING. WELL, MOST THINGS. WE SHOULD VISIT HIS GRAVE.

SHE KNOWS I CAN'T MAKE PROMISES ABOUT THE FUTURE. BUT NEITHER OF US WANTS TO ADMIT THAT.

MAYBE SOMEDAY.

LATER, I PICK UP MEGHAN FROM PRESCHOOL.

KIEREN!

DID YOU HAVE FUN TODAY?

WE HAVE A NEW HAMSTER, SPARKLES. HE'S SHY. AND I HAVE A NEW BEST FRIEND.

WHAT HAPPENED TO DIDI?

SHE'S MY BEST FRIEND, TOO.

OH. VERY DIPLOMATIC OF YOU. WHO'S THE INTERLOPER?

ETHAN.

ISN'T ETHAN A BOY?

YOU'RE A BOY.

I'M NOT A BOY. I'M YOUR BROTHER.

ST. NICHOLAS PRESCHOOL

THANK YOU FOR YOUR GENEROSITY.

IT WAS JUST A GESTURE, REALLY. AFTER ALL, YOU'RE DOING GOD'S WORK. THANK YOU FOR THE TOUR AND FOR YOUR HOSPITALITY.

BRAD?

FANCY MEETING YOU HERE.

AND WHO IS THIS YOUNG LADY?

I'M MEGHAN.

YOU STAY AWAY FROM HER.

KIEREN!

IT'S OKAY, MRS. RAMOS. WE WERE JUST LEAVING.

SO, LET ME GET THIS STRAIGHT: THE BIG BOMBSHELLS THAT YOU'RE GOING TO LAY ON QUINCIE ARE THAT BRAD SHOWED UP AT A FOOTBALL GAME, HELPED YOUR DAD CHANGE A FLAT TIRE, AND GAVE MONEY TO MEGHAN'S PRESCHOOL?

YOU DON'T THINK THAT'S WEIRD?

HE COULD JUST BE MESSING WITH YOU.

OKAY, LET'S ASSUME THE FLAT WAS A COINCIDENCE AND THAT HE'S THE CHARITABLE TYPE, WHICH I *SERIOUSLY* DOUBT.

A HIGH-SCHOOL FOOTBALL GAME? DOESN'T HE HAVE ANY FRIENDS HIS OWN AGE?

UH, KIEREN, THIS IS TEXAS. LOTS OF PEOPLE GO TO THE GAMES.

I DON'T THINK IT SAYS "SERIAL KILLER," AND NEITHER WILL QUINCIE. I GET THAT YOU HAVE ISSUES WITH BRAD, BUT HE'S NOT OUR ONLY SUSPECT. THERE'S STILL DAVIDSON, RUBY, AND MITCH TO THINK ABOUT.

WHY MITCH? BECAUSE HE'S HOMELESS? I LIKE MITCH.

EVERYBODY LIKES MITCH. BUT HE IS A LITTLE –

NO WAY IT'S MITCH. BUT BRAD–

I'M TELLING YOU, THE WAY BRAD'S BEEN SCHMOOZING QUINCIE, YOU'RE GONNA NEED A SMOKING GUN.

THE GIRL AT WORK IS NOTHING LIKE THE ONE YOU'RE ALWAYS TALKING ABOUT.

I'M NOT ALWAYS TALKING ABOUT . . . .

MAYBE I AM. THEY MAY HAVE A POINT ABOUT QUINCIE AND BRAD, TOO. AND I CAN'T LET HIM DISTRACT ME WITH HIS LITTLE GAMES.

THIS WEEKEND, A BODY WAS FOUND ON THE HIKE-AND-BIKE TRAIL ALONGSIDE TOWN LAKE.

THERE'S NO CONFIRMATION FROM APD, BUT SOMEBODY LEAKED TO THE MEDIA THAT THE BODY HAD BEEN DRAINED.

QUINCIE AND HER UNCLE SHOULD BE AT WORK. SO, NOW'S A GOOD TIME FOR Y'ALL TO VAMP-PROOF HER HOUSE. JUST KEEP OUT OF SIGHT.

I WANT TO GO, TOO. BUT I PROMISED TO BABYSIT MEGHAN. AND I NEED MY PARENTS TO THINK I'M LYING LOW.

QUINCIE IS BEYOND PISSED.

SHE FOUND YOU IN HER YARD?

IN HER HOUSE.

WHAT? WHY WERE YOU—

THE FRONT DOOR WAS UNLOCKED, AND TRAVIS INSISTED THAT WE GO INSIDE AND FINISH THE JOB RIGHT. HE'S SERIOUSLY WORRIED ABOUT HER, AND, YOU KNOW, ARMADILLOS ARE ALL ABOUT CHIVALRY.

ANYWAY, WHEN SHE WALKED IN, HE PANICKED AND—

HOW PISSED IS SHE?

HEY, GET IN!

YOU'RE MAD?

CLYDE CALLED ME WHEN HE GOT HOME. I'M SORRY, QUINCIE.

I'M TRYING TO APOLOGIZE.

TRAVIS AND CLYDE WERE IN MY BEDROOM!

THEY WEREN'T SUPPOSED TO DO THAT, JUST GO INTO YOUR HOUSE LIKE THAT.

I DIDN'T CALL QUINCIE LAST NIGHT AFTER THE GUYS LEFT.

I FIGURED IT WOULD BE BETTER TO LET HER COOL DOWN. BUT WHEN SHE'S NOT AT SCHOOL AGAIN IN THE MORNING . . .

I CAN'T HELP BUT WORRY.

I LEAVE MESSAGES FOR HER AT HOME. AT THE RESTAURANT.

WHEN I KNOCK ON THE BACK DOOR OF SANGUINI'S, TRAVIS ANSWERS.

THEY WENT OUT SHOPPING—QUINCIE AND BRAD. THEY'RE STILL LOOKING FOR "VAMPIRE CHEF" DUDS FOR THIS WEEKEND.

HOW WAS SHE TODAY?

LIKE SHE IS MOST DAYS. DRINKING. HANGING ON EVERY WORD HE SAYS.

DRINKING? SHE'S DRINKING MOST DAYS?

AND NIGHTS.

BRAD KEEPS GOING ON ABOUT HOW MUCH HE NEEDS HER HELP. NOT THAT SHE'S DOING MUCH BESIDES HOVERING.

AUSTIN POLICE HAVE ANNOUNCED THAT THEY'RE CLOSE TO MAKING AN ARREST IN THE MURDER OF SANGUINI'S CHEF VAGGIO BIANCHI.

JOEY DIDN'T SHOW TODAY. I CALL HIS HOME NUMBER AND GET HIS BROTHER LUIS.

I'M JOEY'S TUTOR, YOU KNOW, FROM THE AFTER-SCHOOL PROGRAM, AND—

HAVE YOU SEEN HIM? DO YOU KNOW WHERE HE IS? WE TALKED TO THE COPS, BUT . . .

THIS *BABOSO* BOTHERIN' YOU?

NO.

SO HELP ME, IF THE ANSWERS ARE HERE IN MY OWN BEDROOM, AND I DON'T FIND THEM . . .

YOU'RE UP EARLY.

I DIDN'T SLEEP.

IS IT TRUE THAT WEREWOLVES ORIGINALLY CREATED VAMPIRES TO WIPE OUT HUMANITY?

YOU KNOW ABOUT THAT?

AT A SCHOOL IN THE CARPATHIAN MOUNTAINS? IT'S IN A BOOK UPSTAIRS.

THAT WAS A MISTAKE.

THAT IT HAPPENED, OR THAT I FOUND OUT ABOUT IT?

WOLF SCHOLARS ARE DIVIDED ON THE SUBJECT. MOST ASSIGN IT TO MYTH. SOME BLAME THE CATS. OTHERS—

BUT IT'S POSSIBLE.

MANY THINGS ARE POSSIBLE.

YOU'RE QUIET.

AFTER SCHOOL, I DROP OFF CLYDE AT SANGUINI'S AND THEN HEAD TO TRAVIS'S HOUSE. THEY'RE WORKING ALTERNATING DAYS UNTIL THE REOPENING.

WE'RE BOTH QUIET. IT'S CLYDE WHO MAKES ALL THE NOISE.

I FOUND OUT SOMETHING I DIDN'T WANT TO KNOW.

ABOUT?

WOLVES.

I'M NOT EVEN SURE IT'S TRUE.

I'M NOT SURPRISED WHEN QUINCIE IS ABSENT AGAIN.

THE LAUNCH PARTY IS TONIGHT.

WORLD

NEXT MONDAY, WE'LL BE SAYING GOOD-BYE TO HAWTHORNE AND HELLO TO A FEW OF THE EVEN SPOOKIER GOTHIC MASTERS.

AS FOR THIS WEEKEND'S HOMEWORK . . .

Kieren Morales Home work?

DON'T MISS TONIGHT'S BIG GAME! I'LL SEE Y'ALL THERE!

objective response ???

KIEREN, COULD I SPEAK WITH YOU FOR A MOMENT?

themes objectives responses ???

I WAS WONDERING IF YOU'D TALKED TO QUINCIE. I CHECKED WITH THE OFFICE. NO ONE'S CALLED IN.

I WOULDN'T PUT YOU ON THE SPOT LIKE THIS, BUT *STUDENTS* ARE MISSING. PEOPLE ARE DYING.

ONE OF THE YOUNGER CAFETERIA LADIES DIDN'T CLOCK IN THIS MORNING.

QUINCIE IS OKAY. SHE'S JUST BUSY WITH HER FAMILY'S RESTAURANT.

I'M HERE, IF YOU EVER NEED TO TALK.

WHAT IS QUINCIE THINKING? I KNOW THIS PLACE IS HER FAMILY LEGACY. BUT WOULD HER PARENTS AND GRANDPARENTS HAVE REALLY WANTED THIS?

HAPPY B-DAY 60

we love u cu vaggio

MY MOM AND DAD WOULD HAVE A FIT IF THEY KNEW I WAS HERE. NOT TO MENTION MY LAWYER.

OF THE LIKELY SUSPECTS, ONLY "BRADLEY SANGUINI," THE VAMPIRE CHEF, AND DAVIDSON'S GIRLFRIEND ARE NEW ON THE SCENE. I MAY NOT LIKE HIM, BUT I CAN'T RULE HER OUT, EITHER.

TRAVIS ISN'T THE ONLY PERSON SHE CREEPS OUT. THERE'S SOMETHING ABOUT HER.

PREDATOR

PREY

AND UNLIKE BRAD . . .

SHE WAS LIVING IN AUSTIN AT THE TIME OF VAGGIO'S MURDER.

EMPLOYEE APPLICATIONS SHOULD BE ON FILE.

MAYBE THERE'S A CLUE IN THE PAPERWORK.

KIEREN?

BUSTED.

I WAS LOOKING FOR—

IT'S BEEN CRAZY TONIGHT, BUT HEY, THANKS FOR COMING!

OH, IT'S ALMOST MIDNIGHT. WE'VE GOT TO GET TO THE DINING ROOM OR WE'LL MISS BRADLEY'S TOAST. WAIT UNTIL—

SHE'S BEEN DRINKING AGAIN. I HOPE THAT EXPLAINS THE OUTFIT.

QUINCIE, STOP, STOP. I'M HERE TO—

LATER.

MAYBE I WAS WRONG ABOUT RUBY.

BUT QUINCIE, YOU'RE . . . WHEN'S THE LAST TIME YOU SHOWED UP AT SCHOOL? DID YOU KNOW THAT FIVE STUDENTS ARE MISSING? EIGHT OR NINE PEOPLE IN THE NEIGHBORHOOD?

THE COPS—

DON'T UNDERSTAND WHAT THEY'RE UP AGAINST.

THEY KNOW VAGGIO'S MURDERER IS OUT THERE.

OUT THERE.

DO YOU REALIZE HE COULD BE *HERE*, IN THIS VERY BUILDING AT THIS VERY MOMENT?

THAT WAS JUST BRILLIANT! GOD, I HOPE MY PARENTS DON'T HEAR ABOUT IT. AT LEAST I DIDN'T SPOT ANY COPS IN THE DINING ROOM.

HEY, KIEREN!

YOU SEEN TRAVIS? HE DIDN'T SHOW UP FOR WORK.

NOT YET. WHAT HAVE YOU FOUND OUT?

ABOUT RUBY . . . SLUTTY DRESSER, BITCHY PERSONALITY, KILLER BODY . . .

IS THERE A POINT?

SHE'S A WERECAT.

YOU REALLY DIDN'T KNOW SHE WAS A CAT. HOW COULD YOU MISS HER SCENT? WAS IT THE MOON CYCLE?

ANY WOLF WORTH HIS NOSE SHOULD BE ABLE TO SMELL A CAT COMING.

ANY FULL WOLF.

MIDMONTH IS NO EXCUSE. BUT BEING AN OPOSSUM, CLYDE'S NO EXPERT.

IT MUST HAVE BEEN RUBY'S CINNAMON PERFUME. AND NOW THAT I THINK ABOUT IT, SHE'S ALWAYS STANDING DOWNWIND. PLUS, YOU KNOW, MY ALLERGIES HAVE BEEN ACTING UP.

ALLERGIES SUCK.

POLLEN AND MOLD.

CEDAR, MAN. CEDAR IS THE WORST.

I LEFT A MESSAGE ON TRAVIS'S CELL LAST NIGHT. HE SHOULD BE HERE BY NOW.

HOW'S OUR FRIEND, THE VAMPIRE CHEF?

EH, HE'S STILL TOTALLY INTO QUINCIE, TIGHT WITH DAVIDSON. HE DOESN'T BOTHER MUCH WITH ANYONE ELSE.

AND HE WEARS HIS FAKE FANGS AND RED CONTACTS ALL THE TIME. PERSONALLY, I THINK IT'S A SIGN OF INSECURITY. WE'RE TALKING MAJOR ATTENTION HOG, IF YOU KNOW WHAT I MEAN.

ALL OF WHICH KEEPS BRAD OFF MY FAVORITE-PEOPLE LIST, BUT DOESN'T NECESSARILY EQUAL MURDERER.

OH, AND "BRADLEY SANGUINI" IS JUST A STAGE NAME.

I FIGURED OUT THAT MUCH.

HIS REAL NAME'S HENRY JOHNSON.

http://www.m......

Searching

henry johnso

GO

ARE YOU OKAY?

IN THE BACKYARD . . .

STAY WITH CLYDE. I'LL BE RIGHT BACK.

WHAM

THE COPS CALL NOT LONG AFTER I FIND BRAZOS DEAD, NOT LONG AFTER I FIND OUT THAT TRAVIS HAS BEEN MURDERED.

THEY ASK ME TO COME IN. VOLUNTARILY. JUST FOR A FEW QUESTIONS. MY LAWYER AGREES TO MEET ME AT THE STATION.

SO FAR TODAY, I'VE SEEN NO SIGN OF DETECTIVE ZALESKI.

SO, YOU KNEW MR. BIANCHI YOUR WHOLE LIFE. DID YOU TWO EVER ARGUE?

I'VE ALREADY TOLD YOU. . . .

WHY AREN'T YOU OUT TRYING TO CATCH THE KILLER?

KIEREN—

DO YOU HAVE ANYTHING *NEW* TO ASK ME?

WHAT WAS YOUR RELATIONSHIP TO TRAVIS REID?

HE WAS ONE OF MY BEST FRIENDS.

SOMETHING YOU WANT TO TELL ME?

JUST PLAYING IT SAFE.

TRAVIS WAS A GREAT KID, AND I KNOW YOU'RE HURTING, BUT—

CAN I ASK YOU A QUESTION?

SURE.

YOU KNOW HOW SOME PREACHERS SAY THAT THE SNAKE IN EDEN WAS A SHIFTER?

THE CHURCH HAS NO OFFICIAL POSITION ON—

I KNOW, BUT BEFORE YOU MET MOM, DID YOU EVER THINK THE STORY MIGHT BE TRUE?

SINCE WHEN ARE YOU WORRIED ABOUT THAT?

I CAME ACROSS SOMETHING IN MY STUDIES THAT MADE ME WONDER.

KIEREN, OVER THE COURSE OF HISTORY, MANY PEOPLE HAVE TWISTED RELIGION TO JUSTIFY THEIR PREJUDICES.

WHAT I KNOW IN MY HEART IS THAT I LOVE YOUR MOTHER, AND THAT YOU AND YOUR SISTER ARE NOT ONLY OUR CHILDREN BUT ALSO CHILDREN OF GOD.

HAVE FAITH.

SATURDAY NIGHT

I MANAGE TO SWEET-TALK THE HOSTESS INTO SEATING ME.

◆ Sanguini's ◆
A VERY RARE RESTAURANT

PREY MENU
(select one in each category below)

antipasto
portobello mushroom pâté

roasted eggplant oregano

primo
corn conchiglie salad
in virgin olive oil over butterhead lettuce

mozzarella, gorgonzola, and parmesan ravioli
in wild mushroom sauce

secondo
eggplant parmesan

roasted tomato and wild mushroom stew
in red wine sauce and vegetable stock

contorno
roasted asparagus

tomato and heart of palm salad

dolce
tiramisù

crème brûlée

◆ Sanguini's ◆
A VERY RARE RESTAURANT

PREDATOR MENU
(select one in each category below)

antipasto
foie gras terrine
marinated in Cabernet Sauvignon,
sautéed with brandy in balsamic vinegar

veal tartare

primo
breaded pig's feet à la Sanguini's
in Merlot and onion cream sauce with fettuccine Alfredo

sautéed porcini and veal kidneys
in veal stock reduction with orecchiette

secondo
blood and tongue sausages with new potatoes

boar's head pie with boiled eggs in a graham cracker crust

contorno
ham and peas mozzarella

sweetbreads with spinach

dolce
rice pudding blood cakes

chilled baby squirrels simmered in
orange brandy, bathed in honey cream sauce

THE PREDATOR MENU LOOKS FREAKISHLY BLOODY, EVEN TO A WOLF-MAN LIKE ME.

I GUESS THAT'S WHAT THEY'RE GOING FOR, THOUGH. FREAKISHLY BLOODY.

ARE YOU GOING TO ORDER?

IF THIS IS ABOUT RUBY . . .

IT'S NOT.

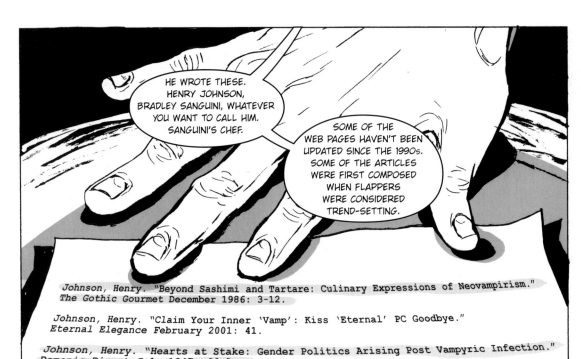

Johnson, Henry. "Beyond Sashimi and Tartare: Culinary Expressions of Neovampirism."
The Gothic Gourmet December 1986: 3-12.

Johnson, Henry. "Claim Your Inner 'Vamp': Kiss 'Eternal' PC Goodbye."
Eternal Elegance February 2001: 41.

Johnson, Henry. "Hearts at Stake: Gender Politics Arising Post Vampyric Infection."
Demonic Digest July 1947: 66:2.

Johnson, Henry. "Rebel Rogues: Eternal Rights in a Dictatorship-Monarchy."
Predators & Politics February 1923: 45:8.

Johnson, Henry. "Sunbelt Migration: Undead Opportunities in the American Southwest
Underworld Business Monthly May 1972: 1:6.

Johnson, Henry. "Vampirism and Attention Deficit Disorder: Ramifications Related
cial Interaction, Cross-Species Relationships, and Iron Deficiency."
ternatural Psychology March/April 1994: 26:2.

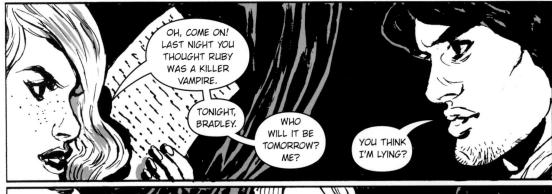

QUINCIE, LOOK AT YOURSELF.

YOU'VE CHANGED. I'M NOT ONLY TALKING ABOUT WARDROBE, THOUGH I MUST SAY—

WHY ARE YOU EVEN HERE? YOU SAID YOU WERE LEAVING.

SO WHAT? YOU'RE TRYING TO BEAT ME TO IT? SHUT ME OUT OF YOUR LIFE?

I'VE BEEN HERE THE WHOLE TIME.

NO, YOU HAVEN'T! I DON'T KNOW WHO YOU ARE.

QUINCIE, THIS GUY YOU'RE MESSING AROUND WITH IS DANGEROUS.

I'M NOT MESSING AROUND WITH—

HE'S EVIL. AND YOU'RE, YOU'RE SLIPPING AWAY.

QUINCIE SEEMS SO SURE THAT BRAD'S INNOCENT, AND SHE'S GOTTEN TO KNOW HIM PRETTY WELL. TOO WELL.

STILL, IT'S A COMMON NAME: HENRY JOHNSON.

AND IF HE THINKS *I'M* THE MURDERER, THAT WOULD EXPLAIN HIS HOSTILITY TOWARD ME. HIS PROTECTIVENESS OF QUINCIE.

GOD, DO I JUST *WANT* HIM TO BE GUILTY BECAUSE I'M JEALOUS?

YO, KIEREN!

AREN'T YOU SUPPOSED TO BE WASHING DISHES?

SCREW THAT. I'M OUT OF THERE FOR GOOD. HAVE YOU BEEN HOME TONIGHT? TALKED TO YOUR PARENTS?

NO, I—

MY MOM CALLED. SHE WENT TO DROP OFF A CASSEROLE AT TRAVIS'S HOUSE.

MY DAD MADE TAMALES—

RIGHT. AND THEY RAN INTO EACH OTHER, AND YOUR DAD SAID THE COPS ARE LOOKING FOR YOU. LISTEN . . .

WHAT?

OBJECTS IN MIRROR ARE CLOSER THAN THEY APPEAR

GET IN.

I WAS AT TRAVIS'S HOUSE, TALKING TO HIS AUNTIE, AND IT TURNS OUT THAT A WERECAT KILLED HIM.

RUBY.

TRAVIS WAS A PREY SHIFTER. RUBY, A PREDATOR. BUT SHIFTER-ON-SHIFTER MURDERS ARE RARE.

SHE MAY HAVE KILLED TRAVIS—

AND VAGGIO AND—

WE NEED PROOF.

KIEREN, LET IT GO. YOUR TIME IS UP.

MEANING *WHAT*, EXACTLY?

LET ME GUESS. THE LOCATION OF THE WOLF PACK?

YOUR DAD SAID NOT TO GO HOME AGAIN.

I NEVER GOT TO SAY GOOD-BYE.

YOU'RE NOT GOING TO LOOK AT IT? AREN'T YOU DYING TO KNOW WHERE THE PACK IS?

YES. NO.

THAT CAN WAIT. I CAN'T LEAVE YET, ANYWAY. I HAVE TO TALK TO QUINCIE, TO MAKE HER UNDERSTAND.

AGAIN? LOOK, YOU'VE TRIED AND—

YOU'RE GOING TO TRY AGAIN. I RESPECT THAT. I DO.

I'M GOING TO ASK HER TO LEAVE TOWN WITH ME.

WOLF OR NO, RIGHT NOW I'M LESS OF A DANGER TO HER THAN WHAT SHE'S FACING HERE.

ARE YOU SERIOUS? WHAT WITH THE PACK AND YOUR WOLFY-NESS AND HER BEING ALL HUMAN AND THE MURDERS AND THE COPS AND SANGUINI'S . . .

THAT'S A GREAT IDEA. KICK-ASS. REALLY.

IT WAS A MISTAKE, TRYING TO TALK TO QUINCIE WHILE SHE WAS BUSY WORKING. I'LL CATCH HER ON HER WAY HOME.

BITCH.

RUBY.

UM, I DIDN'T MEAN, LIKE, WOLF BITCH. LIKE YOUR MOM. I MEANT . . .

I KNOW WHAT YOU MEANT.

TRAVIS'S FAMILY PUT OUT A HIT ON HER. THEY'RE A BIG DEAL IN THE ARMADILLO WORLD, YOU KNOW.

IT'S NEWS TO ME. I GUESS WE ALL HAVE OUR SECRETS.

DO YOU SEE QUINCIE?

NUH-UH.

THERE HE IS, THE VAMPIRE CHEF.

BUT WHERE'S SHE?

LATER

DO YOU WANT TO PLAY CARDS?

DO YOU HAVE CARDS?

NO.

MUCH LATER

I HOPE QUINCIE WILL BE MORE REASONABLE IN THE LIGHT OF DAY.

WE'RE KIND OF CONSPICUOUS OUT HERE. AND BY *WE*, I MEAN *YOU*.

I DON'T THINK HER CELL IS TURNED ON.

THAT'S NICE. CAN I HAVE MY PHONE BACK?

HANG ON, I'M TRYING HER LANDLINE.

NOBODY'S PICKING UP.

QUINCIE? IT'S ME. I THOUGHT YOU MIGHT BE HURTIN' THIS MORNING. TOO MUCH TO DRINK, HUH? LOOK, FORGET LAST NIGHT. I WAS UPSET. I'D LOVE TO TALK ONCE YOU'VE SOBERED UP. GIVE ME A CALL.

NICE AND BREEZY, ROMEO.

HOWDY, MITCH! HAVE YOU SEEN QUINCIE?

NOPE. SO– SORRY, BOY. NO QUINCIE SO FAR TODAY.

HOMELESS INDIE PRO-LIFE VAMPIRE NEEDS BLOOD

BRAD'S GOONS—IAN AND JEROME, THE ONES WHO "ESCORTED" ME OUT OF SANGUINI'S.

WHERE'S QUINCIE MORRIS? I RECOGNIZE HER SCENT.

SURE, *QUINCIE* HE CAN SMELL, ALLERGIES OR NO ALLERGIES.

WEIRD. THEY SEEM AFRAID OF ME.

BRADLEY TOOK HER AWAY.

WE DON'T KNOW WHERE.

WHAT?

HUH?

THEY'RE BIRDS.

VULTURES.

CLYDE IS RIGHT. I CAN SMELL IT, SEE IT NOW. THESE TWO ARE WERESCAVENGERS, BRADLEY'S "EYES IN THE SKY." FOR THE OBVIOUS REASON, VULTURES ARE KNOWN TO TRAIL AFTER BLOODSUCKERS.

THIS PROVES IT. QUINCIE'S MAKE-BELIEVE VAMPIRE CHEF ISN'T SO MAKE-BELIEVE AFTER ALL.

I'M A WOLF. YOU GOT THAT? A WOLF.

NOW, WHAT DO YOU KNOW?

WILL YOU KILL US?

BECAUSE THE VAMPIRE WOULD DO WORSE.

BUT WE ARE STILL WEREPEOPLE.

WE WILL LEAVE HIS SERVICE NOW.

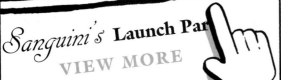

VICE PRINCIPAL HARDING. SINCE WHEN DOES *HE* LIKE TO PLAY VAMPIRE?

I'VE GOT A LEAD AT SCHOOL. QUINCIE, IF YOU GET THIS MESSAGE, I SWEAR I'M GOING TO FIND YOU.

I TAKE IT AS A GOOD SIGN THAT I'M NOT ARRESTED IN THE PARKING LOT.

I'M HERE TO SEE MR. HARDING. IT'S KIND OF AN EMERGENCY.

HE'LL BE OUT MOST OF THE DAY.

WHAT AM I SUPPOSED TO DO?

SORRY, MA'AM. KIEREN'S JUST FREAKED ABOUT HIS QUIZ TODAY. YOU KNOW HOW BRAINIACS ARE. STRESS, STRESS, STRESS. OUR BOY'S SHOOTING FOR VALEDICTORIAN, AFTER ALL.

MR. HARDING SHOULD BE BACK AROUND TWO THIRTY. IF HE HAS A FEW MINUTES, I'LL SEND FOR YOU.

AT FIRST I HOPE QUINCIE MIGHT SHOW UP AT SCHOOL TODAY.

BUT SHE ISN'T AT HER LOCKER BEFORE THE BELL.

OR, LATER, IN ENGLISH.

AS LONG AS I'M HERE, I MIGHT AS WELL DO MY HOMEWORK ON THE VICE PRINCIPAL.

WHERE'S QUINCIE TODAY?

SHE'S REALLY MISSING NOW, NOT JUST ABSENT FROM SCHOOL.

SEE ME AFTER CLASS.

HAS QUINCIE'S UNCLE CONTACTED THE POLICE?

I'M NOT SURE.

NOT SURE ABOUT THAT. NOT SURE IF I SHOULD SAY WHAT I'M ABOUT TO, EITHER. BUT I'M TIRED OF CHASING MY TAIL, AND I THINK I CAN TRUST MRS. LEVY.

THIS MAY SOUND STRANGE, BUT I THINK MR. HARDING KNOWS SOMETHING ABOUT WHAT HAPPENED TO QUINCIE. TO HER, AND THE OTHER MISSING STUDENTS, AND THE CAFETERIA LADY.

YOU'RE A SMART GUY, KIEREN. VERY SMART.

I THINK YOU'LL UNDERSTAND WHEN I SAY THERE ARE THREE THINGS TO KEEP IN MIND WHEN IT COMES TO OUR VICE PRINCIPAL.

ONE: HE'S A TOTAL HARD-ASS ABOUT STANDARDIZED TESTING. TWO: HE HAS A BATTLE-AXE MOUNTED ON HIS OFFICE WALL. AND THREE: HE'S AN UNDEAD, BLOODSUCKING FIEND.

VICE PRINCIPAL HARDING

WE SNEAK THROUGH THE BACK-HALL DOOR TO HARDING'S OFFICE.

HE HAS A MESSAGE ON HIS DESK FROM THE COPS, SAYING TO CALL IF I SHOW UP AT SCHOOL TODAY, AND A MESSAGE FROM HIS ASSISTANT, SAYING THAT I DID.

VICE PRINCIPAL HARDING

SOMETHING'S GOING DOWN.

IF YOU DON'T HEAR FROM ME AGAIN, I JUST WANT YOU TO KNOW THAT I—

HE'S HERE!

SORRY, QUINCIE. I GOTTA GO.

VICE PRINCIPAL
HARDING

THE SILVER-BULLET-WEREWOLF THING?

MYTH.

MR. MORALES?

THE ONLY WAYS TO DESTROY A *VAMPIRE* ARE . . .

FIRE.
HOLY WATER.
IMPALING THE HEART.

BEHEADING.

WHERE'S QUINCIE MORRIS?

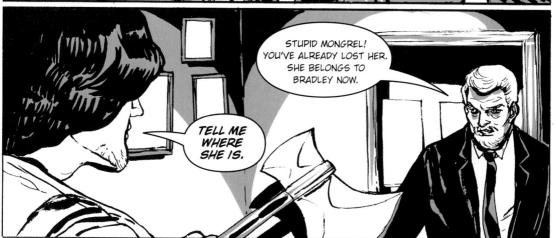

STUPID MONGREL! YOU'VE ALREADY LOST HER. SHE BELONGS TO BRADLEY NOW.

TELL ME WHERE SHE IS.

YOU FORGET WHO I AM. WHAT YOU ARE.

I'M SURE THE POLICE WOULD BE INTERESTED TO KNOW THAT THEIR PRIME MURDER SUSPECT IS ARMED ON SCHOOL GROUNDS.

I'M SURE THE MEDIA WOULD LOVE TO KNOW THAT A FAMILY OF WEREWOLVES IS TERRORIZING THE CITY.

YOU'RE NOT WORTH SULLYING MY HANDS.

I CAN JUST SEE IT. THE UNIVERSITY WILL FIRE YOUR FATHER. THE VICTIMS' FAMILIES WILL HANG YOUR MOTHER. THE AUTHORITIES WILL TOSS YOUR BABY SISTER IN A CAGE.

AND YOU— THEY'LL GUN YOU DOWN LIKE THE DOG YOU ARE.

YOU KNOW, I'VE WANTED TO DO THAT SINCE BEFORE HE WAS A VAMPIRE.

IS IT OVER?

WHAT ARE WE GOING TO DO ABOUT HIM?

THIS SHOULD POINT THE MEDICAL EXAMINER IN THE RIGHT DIRECTION.

Vampire

NOW, WHAT'S THIS ABOUT YOUR BEING A WEREWOLF?

CLYDE, SHE WAS RIGHT OUTSIDE THE DOOR.

WEREWOLF? HA! YOU THINK HE'S BADASS ENOUGH TO BE A WEREWOLF?

LET'S TAKE THIS DISCUSSION ELSEWHERE.

AFTER THE "FIRE DRILL," MRS. LEVY SENDS THE REST OF HER CLASSES TO THE LIBRARY.

I ADMIT TO BEING A WOLF, BUT NOT A HYBRID, AND I DON'T MENTION THAT MY PARENTS THINK I'VE ALREADY LEFT FOR THE PACK.

AND SO WE KNOW THAT BRAD'S A VAMPIRE.

AND THAT HARDING WAS A VAMPIRE.

AS A WERECAT, RUBY'S A BIG QUESTION MARK.

SHE'S A BIG QUESTION MARK WHO MAYBE MURDERED TRAVIS.

THAT POOR BOY.

WE CAN'T BE SURE WHAT TO THINK ABOUT QUINCIE'S UNCLE DAVIDSON.

HAVE YOU TRIED TO WARN HIM? THE UNCLE?

HAVEN'T HAD A CHANCE. I'VE LEFT PHONE MESSAGES.

NO ONE'S BEEN HOME WHEN WE'VE STOPPED BY.

WU DELIVERS

SO, FOR ALL WE KNOW, QUINCIE COULD BE AT THE RESTAURANT NOW. WHAT TIME DOES THE PLACE OPEN?

SUNSET. THAT'S WHAT? ABOUT SEVEN THIRTY, SEVEN FORTY?

WHAT ARE Y'ALL TALKING ABOUT? WE CAN'T GO BACK THERE.

QUINCIE DISAPPEARED AT SANGUINI'S. VAGGIO *DIED* AT SANGUINI'S. THE PLACE IS CRAWLING WITH MONSTERS!

THE FIRST TIME I WENT, BRAD MADE A HUGE SCENE IN THE MIDDLE OF HIS TOAST. THE SECOND TIME, THE BOUNCERS ESCORTED ME OUT.

I JUST WANT TO FIND QUINCIE, IF SHE'S THERE, AND GET HER OUT SAFE. YOU KNOW, FAST, QUIET, LOW PROFILE.

AND HOW EXACTLY ARE YOU PLANNING TO PULL OFF THAT LITTLE MIRACLE?

I HAVE AN IDEA.

THE BUZZ AROUND THIS PLACE IS CRAZY.
MRS. LEVY HAS TO BUY US A RESERVATION ON EBAY.

ARE YOU PREDATOR OR PREY?

GOD, THIS IS TEDIOUS.

PREDATOR.

PREDATOR.

OMNIVORE.

WELL, IT'S TRUE.

IT'S SO TEMPTING: GRAB A KNIFE AND CHARGE BRAD HEAD-ON.

BUT HE'S AT LEAST AS STRONG AS I AM. AT LEAST AS FAST. I'D BE OUTNUMBERED, PROBABLY ARRESTED.

I HAVE TO THINK OF MY FAMILY.

OFFICE

KNOCK NOK

OF QUINCIE.

RESTROOMS ARE DOWN THE HALL.

I ALMOST ASK DAVIDSON WHERE QUINCIE IS. I ALMOST WARN HIM OF THE DANGER.

BUT IF CLYDE CAN SMELL THE CAT ON RUBY, MAYBE SHE CAN SMELL THE WOLF ON ME. AND GOD KNOWS I CAN'T TRUST HER.

NO LUCK. LET'S GET OUT OF HERE.

WHEN CLYDE ASKS TO SWING BY THE MAKESHIFT SHRINE FOR TRAVIS, I CAN'T SAY NO.

WE CAN ONLY STAY A FEW MINUTES, BUT I'M GLAD WE CAME.

DETECTIVE ZALESKI.

WE SHOULD GET OUT OF HERE.

DID YOU SEE THAT BIG DUDE?

HE'S A COP, AN OLD FRIEND OF MY MOM'S. HE'S INVESTIGATING WHAT HAPPENED TO THE MISSING STUDENTS. AND TO VAGGIO.

DID HE SEE US?

I THINK SO.

WHAT DOES HE LOOK LIKE TO YOU?

WEREBEAR, OBVIOUSLY.

YOU THINK HE'S THE ONE WHO TIPPED OFF YOUR PARENTS ABOUT THE COPS COMING AFTER YOU?

YEAH, BUT WHY WOULD HE DO THAT? AND WHY JUST LET ME WALK AWAY TONIGHT?

WELL, IF THIS ZALESKI HAS FIGURED OUT THAT THE KILLER IS A VAMPIRE, AND IF HE KNOWS YOU'RE A SHIFTER, THEN HE ALSO KNOWS YOU'RE NOT GUILTY.

BUT HE CAN'T TELL THE OTHER COPS WITHOUT OUTING YOU AND YOUR WHOLE FAMILY. AND, YOU KNOW, HE'S TRYING TO PASS FOR HUMAN HIMSELF.

NOT BAD. ANY NEW THEORIES ON THE MURDERER?

ONLY THAT THERE MAY BE MORE THAN ONE.

I THINK IT OVER. VAGGIO MURDERED AT SANGUINI'S. STUDENTS AND STAFF MISSING FROM THE HIGH SCHOOL. BODIES ON THE LAKEFRONT. BUT NONE OF THE STUDENTS HAVE BEEN FOUND AMONG THE DEAD.

YOU MAY BE RIGHT.

THAT'S YOUR TRUCK!

THAT'S QUINCIE DRIVING IT!

Endless Love BRIDAL PLANNING

QUINCIE WAS DRIVING THIS WAY, AND ACCORDING TO THE RADIO NEWS, A THIRD BODY WAS FOUND AT THE LAKEFRONT.

IT DOESN'T MAKE SENSE. IF THE WEREVULTURES ARE DISPOSING OF BRAD'S KILLS, WHO'S THE SLOPPY MONSTER HAUNTING THIS TRAIL?

AT SUNSET, THE MEXICAN FREE-TAILED BATS CAREEN OUT FROM BENEATH THE CONGRESS AVENUE BRIDGE. BY NOW, THEY'RE ALL OFF HUNTING.

AREN'T THEY?

YOU'RE SUPPOSED TO BEHEAD THEM.

YOU'RE WELCOME. AND I *TRIED*. THIS AXE IS HEAVIER THAN IT LOOKS.

NO, NO, NOT ME. *I* DIDN'T KILL MISS QUINCIE.

BUT YOU KILLED VAGGIO?

NOPE, NOT ME NEITHER. VAGGIO WAS A GOOD, GOOD COOK. LOVED HIS SAUSAGE LASAGNA. AND MEATBALL SANDWICHES.

I'VE ALWAYS LIKED MITCH. BACK WHEN HE WAS HUMAN, ANYWAY.

BUT THE HIKE-AND-BIKE TRAIL IS STILL A VAMPIRE KILLING GROUND. AND, SO FAR AS I CAN TELL, HE'S THE ONLY BLOODSUCKER AROUND.

NOW, NOW, BOY.

DON'T YOU BE
DOIN', DON'T
DO THAT.

I'LL BE
GOOD. BETTER,
I PROMISE.

I'LL JUST
TAKE THE TOURISTS,
THE PEOPLE FROM THE
SUBURBS.

THE ONES WHO WEAR
HAIRSPRAAAAAAAAAAAAAY!

KASPLASH

I THOUGHT
HE WAS GOING
TO STOP.

SO
DID I!

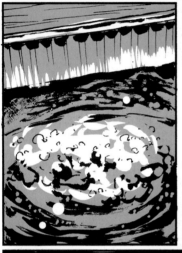

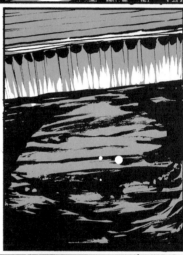

CAN A VAMPIRE DROWN?

DOUBT IT. THEY DON'T NEED TO BREATHE.

HOW MUCH DO YOU THINK HE HAD TO DRINK TONIGHT?

BLOOD OR BEER?

I WAS THINKING BOOZE.

WHAT DO YOU WANT TO DO ABOUT HIM?

HE ISN'T MY PRIORITY.

I DON'T HAVE THE HEART TO HUNT MITCH DOWN. NOT YET.

AFTER SEARCHING A GOOD STRETCH OF THE LAKEFRONT, WE'RE ON OUR WAY TO QUINCIE'S HOUSE. AGAIN.

IT'S ALMOST TWO O'CLOCK IN THE MORNING. THAT'S WHEN SANGUINI'S CLOSES.

Endless Love BRIDAL PLANNING

IF QUINCIE ISN'T AT HOME, I'LL TRY TO TALK TO HER UNCLE, WHETHER HE'S WITH RUBY OR NOT.

THAT WAS A GUNSHOT!

BLAM!

STAY IN THE VAN!

'KAY.

CRASH

IT CAME FROM THE BACK OF THE HOUSE.

OOF!

IT'S RUBY! SHE'S BEEN SHOT.

PART OF ME WANTS TO HELP HER. PART OF ME WANTS TO MAKE HER PAY FOR WHAT SHE DID TO TRAVIS.

BUT EVEN WOUNDED, IN ANIMAL FORM, SHE'S TOO FAST.

GONE.

QUINCIE!

THEY'RE HEADING TOWARD SANGUINI'S.

WHAT FREAKED CLYDE INTO SHIFTING?

NO!

IT'S HORRIBLE.
THE DIFFERENCE BETWEEN US.

BUT SHE'S STILL
MY QUINCIE.

CLYDE HAS BEEN THE PICTURE OF BRAVERY, AT LEAST BY THE POSSUM STANDARD.

BUT SEEING QUINCIE VAMPED OUT HAS KICKED HIM INTO SHOCK-AND-AWE TERRITORY. HE'S OUTTA HERE.

TRUTH IS, EVEN *MY* INSTINCTS ARE SCREAMING. QUINCIE SEEMS SEXIER THAN EVER BEFORE. BUT SHE'S ALSO FREAKING TERRIFYING.

FIRST YOU STEAL MY TRUCK. NOW HE'S STEALING MY VAN.

WITH THE AXE STILL IN IT.

YOU CAN HAVE THE TRUCK BACK. BUT BE CAREFUL. THE POLICE—

I KNOW. I'M A WANTED WOLF-MAN, AND IF I'M ARRESTED . . .

I HAVE TO THINK OF MY MOTHER, AND MEGHAN. I PROMISED MY PARENTS I'D LEAVE TONIGHT.

IT'S A LIE. I WAS SUPPOSED TO HAVE LEFT FORTY-EIGHT HOURS AGO. BUT I DON'T WANT QUINCIE BLAMING HERSELF FOR WHATEVER MAY HAPPEN TO ME.

JUST GO NOW. BE SAFE.

FIRST TELL ME WHAT HAPPENED. TELL ME EVERYTHING.

THERE'S NO TIME! HE'S—

QUINCIE, PLEASE.

HER STORY POURS OUT.

I SPENT SATURDAY NIGHT PASSED OUT ON THE BREAK-ROOM COUCH AT SANGUINI'S.

ON SUNDAY MORNING, I WENT TO BRADLEY'S HOUSE.

AND WE TALKED AND DRANK. HAIR OF THE DOG, HE SAID.

HE SLIPPED SOME KIND OF DRUG INTO THE WINE—AND HE'S BEEN DOSING ME WITH HIS OWN BLOOD FOR, WELL, ABOUT A MONTH. LONG ENOUGH TO TRIGGER THE TRANSFORMATION.

IT WAS IN THE WINE, THE MARINARA SAUCE . . . I DON'T KNOW WHAT-ALL.

THE BLOOD DID MORE THAN TURN ME INTO THIS . . . THING. IT'S BEEN MAKING ME CRAZY. KIEREN, THE WAY I'VE BEEN ACTING LATELY—

IT WASN'T YOUR FAULT. GO ON.

HE KEPT ME IN THE BASEMENT. I SLEPT . . . MOSTLY.

HE WARNED ME OF WHAT I WAS BECOMING. REVEALED WHO AND WHAT THEY ARE.

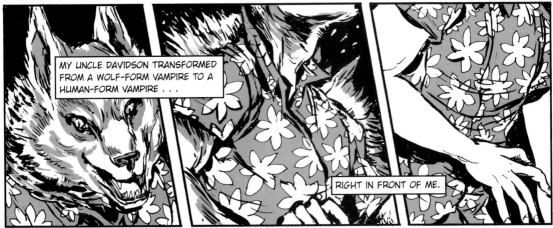

MY UNCLE DAVIDSON TRANSFORMED FROM A WOLF-FORM VAMPIRE TO A HUMAN-FORM VAMPIRE . . .

RIGHT IN FRONT OF ME.

HE WAS IN ON IT THE WHOLE TIME. I THINK HE BECAME UNDEAD WILLINGLY, THAT HE WAS PLAYING MATCHMAKER BETWEEN ME AND BRADLEY.

UNCLE D SAID HE WANTED TO REBUILD OUR FAMILY SO IT WOULD LAST. YOU KNOW, FOREVER.

DAVIDSON DID TAKE IT HARD WHEN YOUR DAD DIED.

RUBY *IS* A SPY, AN ASSASSIN.

SHE WAS SHOT.

WE DON'T HAVE TO WORRY ABOUT UNCLE D ANYMORE. RUBY STAKED HIM TONIGHT.

THAT WAS ME. I FOUND GRAMPA CRIMI'S GUN IN UNCLE D'S NIGHTSTAND. LATER ON, SHE ATTACKED ME. I DIDN'T HAVE A CHOICE.

I BELIEVE YOU.

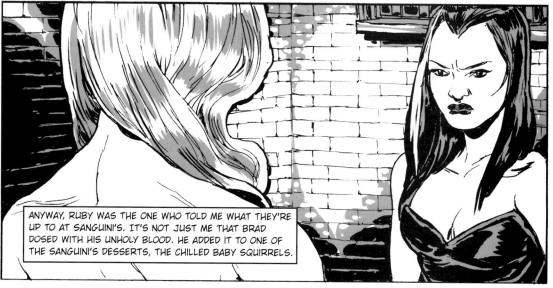

ANYWAY, RUBY WAS THE ONE WHO TOLD ME WHAT THEY'RE UP TO AT SANGUINI'S. IT'S NOT JUST ME THAT BRAD DOSED WITH HIS UNHOLY BLOOD. HE ADDED IT TO ONE OF THE SANGUINI'S DESSERTS, THE CHILLED BABY SQUIRRELS.

YOU COULD RUN AWAY WITH ME.

KIEREN . . .

BRADLEY IS USING MY RESTAURANT TO CREATE NEW VAMPIRES. I'LL TORCH THE PLACE BEFORE I LET HIM GO ON DOING THAT, BUT YOU—

I'M NOT LEAVING UNTIL YOU'RE FREE OF THAT MONSTER. HE KILLED . . .

YOU.

HE *KILLED* YOU.

SAME PLAN.

EXCEPT I'LL PLAY THE VICTIM INSTEAD OF CLYDE.

WHEN BRAD MOVES IN TO FEED, I CAN TAKE HIM.

THAT TIME AT THE RAILROAD TRACKS, IT WAS MY SELF-PRESERVATION INSTINCT KICKING IN. IT'LL KICK IN AGAIN.

I'LL PRETEND TO BE A WILLING SACRIFICE AND THEN SURPRISE HIM WITH MY CLAWS.

DO YOU THINK HE'LL FALL FOR THAT? HE KNOWS WHAT YOU ARE.

IF HE DOESN'T, HE DOESN'T. YOU JUST STAY OUT OF THE WAY.

WHAT ABOUT THE BODYGUARDS?

THEY'RE WEREVULTURES.

I'VE TALKED TO THEM, WEREPERSON TO WEREPERSON. THEY WON'T INTERFERE.

CLYDE TOLD ME ALL WEREPEOPLE HATE VAMPIRES.

NOTHING IS THAT SIMPLE, NOT ANYMORE.

BRAD'S BEEN RUNNING THE WHOLE SHOW.

UNTIL NOW.

BABY, YOU'RE LATE.

I BROUGHT THE "BEVERAGE" YOU ASKED FOR.

PITY YOU DIDN'T SELECT A LOVELIER BOUQUET.

BUT, I ADMIT, THIS GESTURE, IT'S A TREMENDOUS SHOW OF YOUR CHANGING LOYALTIES.

I'M TOUCHED.

ROUGH DAY AT SCHOOL, BOY? I HEAR SOMEBODY BEHEADED THE VICE PRINCIPAL. AND NOW THIS. SACRIFICING YOUR LIFE FOR QUINCIE. I'M IMPRESSED.

GO AHEAD, BABY! LADIES FIRST.

YOU WANT *ME* TO BITE *HIM*?

SO MUCH FOR THE PLAN.

174

FORGOT HE COULD TURN INTO MIST.

THUD

YOU'RE SAYING YOU'LL GIVE UP? LEAVE US ALONE? YOU THINK I'M THAT CLUELESS?

QUINCIE, YOU CAN'T NEGOTIATE WITH—

THINK OF THE DRAMA. THAT'S WHAT SANGUINI'S IS ALL ABOUT, ISN'T IT?

WHAT'S THE POINT IN LETTING YOU TASTE HIM IF THE STAKES AREN'T ALL OR NOTHING?

AND BESIDES, WOLVES DON'T LIVE THAT LONG, NOT EVEN AS LONG AS HUMANS. BUT WE'LL STILL BE HERE.

YOU'LL ABANDON SANGUINI'S? LEAVE AUSTIN?

HE'S LYING BY OMISSION— LEAVING OUT THE KEY DETAIL.

HE *KNOWS* SHE CAN'T WIN.

UNTIL THEIR FIRST KILL, VAMPIRES CAN'T HIDE BEHIND A HUMAN FACE, AND QUINCIE WOULDN'T LOOK LIKE THAT IF SHE HAD A CHOICE.

ACCORDING TO MY WERESTUDIES, VAMPIRES ALWAYS DRAIN THEIR FIRST VICTIM TO DEATH.

THEY CAN'T HELP THEMSELVES. THE INITIAL BLOODLUST IS A KIND OF INSANITY.

OVERWHELMING. ALL-CONSUMING. THE DEMONIC SIDE TAKES CONTROL.

THIS IS THE MOST FUN I'VE HAD IN AGES.

BUT BRAD DOESN'T KNOW QUINCIE LIKE I DO. HE DOESN'T BELIEVE IN HER LIKE I DO.

IF SHE NEEDS TO PROVE THAT SHE CAN DO THIS, THAT SHE'S NOT A MONSTER, I PROBABLY UNDERSTAND THAT BETTER THAN ANYBODY.

I'LL GLADLY OFFER MY THROAT TO HER FANGS.

BUT MY INNER WOLF HAS OTHER PLANS.

GET IT OVER WITH. QUINCIE, GET IT OVER—

GET BACK!

OR MAYBE I SHOULD KILL HIM BEFORE HE SHREDS YOU INTO DAMP, BROKEN BITS.

YOU SEE HOW DOOMED IT IS, BABY. YOUR SORRY ADOLESCENT FLING.

THINK FOR A MOMENT. VAMPIRE-WOLF? VAMPIRE-VAMPIRE? THE ANSWER IS OBVIOUS.

THIS ISN'T LIKE THAT EVENING ON THE RAILROAD BRIDGE. MY WOLF HAS BEEN TRAPPED FOR TOO LONG.

NO!

FORGIVE US.

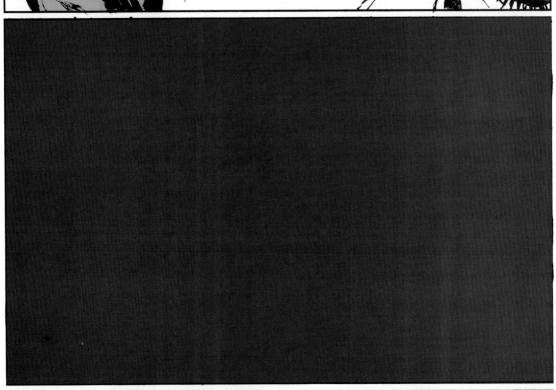

I'M ALIVE.
ALIVE.

AND LOOKING AT THE
ANSWER TO MY PRAYERS.

BABY?

QUINCIE.

I'M HERE.

IT'S TRUE. VAMPIRE OR NOT, SHE'S STILL *QUINCIE.* WE'VE WON THIS ROUND.

ADIÓS. ADDIO. GOOD-BYE.

GOOD RIDDANCE.

For Ginger
C. L. S.

For my mother and father
M. D.

Text copyright © 2011 by Cynthia Leitich Smith
Interior illustrations copyright © 2011 by Ming Doyle

First edition 2011

Library of Congress Cataloging-in-Publication Data

Smith, Cynthia Leitich.
Tantalize : Kieren's story / Cynthia Leitich Smith ;
[illustrations by Ming Doyle]. —1st ed.
p.   cm.
Summary: Werewolf-in-training Kieren is torn between joining
an urban wolf pack and staying to protect his human best friend
(and love interest) Quincie, whose restaurant is in danger
of morphing into a vampire lair.
ISBN 978-0-7636-4114-6
1. Graphic novels. [1. Graphic novels. 2. Werewolves—Fiction.
3. Vampires—Fiction. 4. Supernatural—Fiction.
5. Austin (Tex.)—Fiction.] I. Doyle, Ming, ill. II. Title.
PZ7.7.S6Tan 2011
[Fic]—dc22   2010043152

11 12 13 14 15 16 RRW 10 9 8 7 6 5 4 3 2 1

Printed in Willard, OH, U.S.A.

This book was typeset in CCWildWords.
The illustrations were done in ink.

Candlewick Press
99 Dover Street
Somerville, Massachusetts 02144

visit us at www.candlewick.com

Author's Note

My literary inspiration for *Tantalize* was Abraham "Bram" Stoker's classic novel *Dracula* (1897). As I was rereading the story, it caught my imagination that Stoker's vampires could take the form of wolves, and I decided it would be interesting to write a murder mystery in which the central question was whether a vampire in wolf form or a werewolf was the killer.

Beyond that, *Dracula* had a Texas tie in the character Quincey Morris, one of Van Helsing's original vampire hunters. So, I moved the mythology tradition to my home city of Austin, and named Kieren's best friend Quincie in honor of the original.

Austinites will note that, within the near south and central setting, the novel adds a few streets, businesses, and residences. As tantalizing as it may be to visit Kieren's house or to swing by Sanguini's, such locales exist only within the books.

Finally, I offer a midnight toast to the supernaturally talented Ming Doyle, preternaturally brilliant Deborah Wayshak, and the spooky-cool crews at both Candlewick Press and Curtis Brown, Ltd. Special cheers to Liz Zembruski for her editorial assistance and Sherry Fatla for her design expertise.

That's it for now. Y'all take care. *Adiós. Addio.* Good-bye.

Illustrator's Note

While I have always been grateful to be a member of a profession that so regularly mixes mythic archetypes with pop culture staples, never in my most hopeful imaginings did I think that someday I would be able to spend almost two hundred sequential pages in the fraught yet charming company of a teen wolf.

I can't thank Cynthia and everyone at Candlewick enough for allowing me the honor and pleasure of translating such a thrilling world of monsters, critters, heart-throbs, and hell-raisers into ink and panels.

I'm also indebted to Eric Canete for taking the time to talk process and comic book philosophy, to Kevin Church for being an unflaggingly stalwart source of support and wealth of noir knowledge, and to Neil Cicierega for his many superheroic deeds of word ballooning, encouragement, patience, and belief. It's been a graveyard smash!

Also by best-selling author Cynthia Leitich Smith:

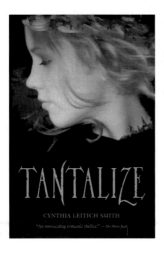

TANTALIZE

Are you predator or prey?
The novel that started it all. . . .

"Smith juices up YA horror with this
intoxicating romantic thriller."
— *The Horn Book*

Hardcover ISBN: 978-0-7636-2791-1
Paperback ISBN: 978-0-7636-4059-0
E-book ISBN: 978-0-7636-5152-7

ETERNAL

At last, Miranda is the life of the party:
all she had to do was die.

A *New York Times* Bestseller

"A true page-turner." — *Dallas Morning News*

Hardcover ISBN: 978-0-7636-3573-2
Paperback ISBN: 978-0-7636-4773-5
E-book ISBN: 978-0-7636-5153-4

BLESSED

Quincie P. Morris is in the fight of her life —
or undeath — as the casts of *Tantalize* and *Eternal*
unite for a clash with the ultimate bloodsucker.

"A hearty meal for the thinking vampire reader."
— *The Horn Book*

Hardcover ISBN: 978-0-7636-4326-3
E-book ISBN: 978-0-7636-5448-1